The Elephant and the Rainbow

Written by Keith Faulkner
Illustrated by Jonathan Lambert

Longmeadow Press

"Oh why am I so dull and gray?"
The elephant sadly said,

As she looked up high and saw
The parrots flying overhead.

As she went along she saw the lion
With his golden mane.

But it made her sad, as she only
Thought of her own gray skin again.

"I wish that I had spots or stripes,"
She told the tall giraffe.

The giraffe just turned her head away
And pretended not to laugh.

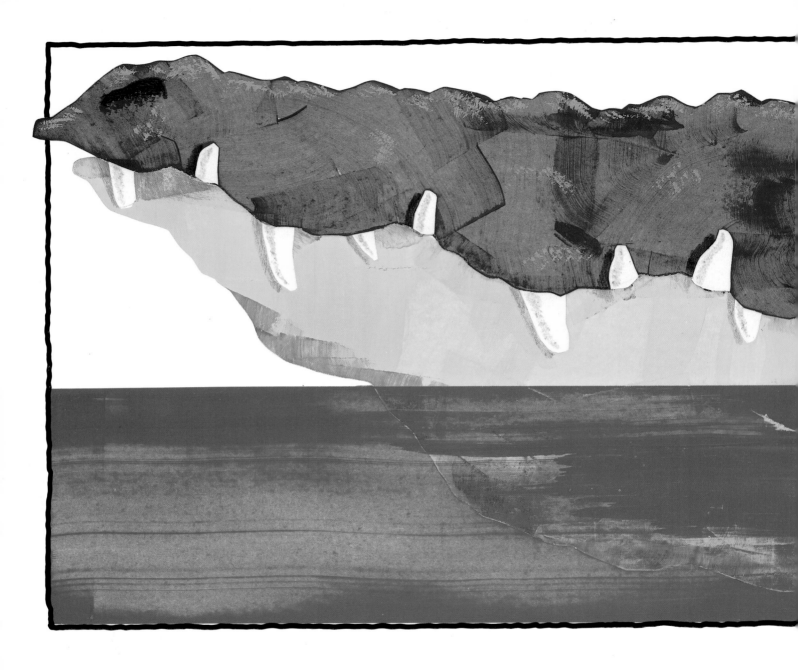

"You've got such lovely emerald scales,"
She told the crocodile.

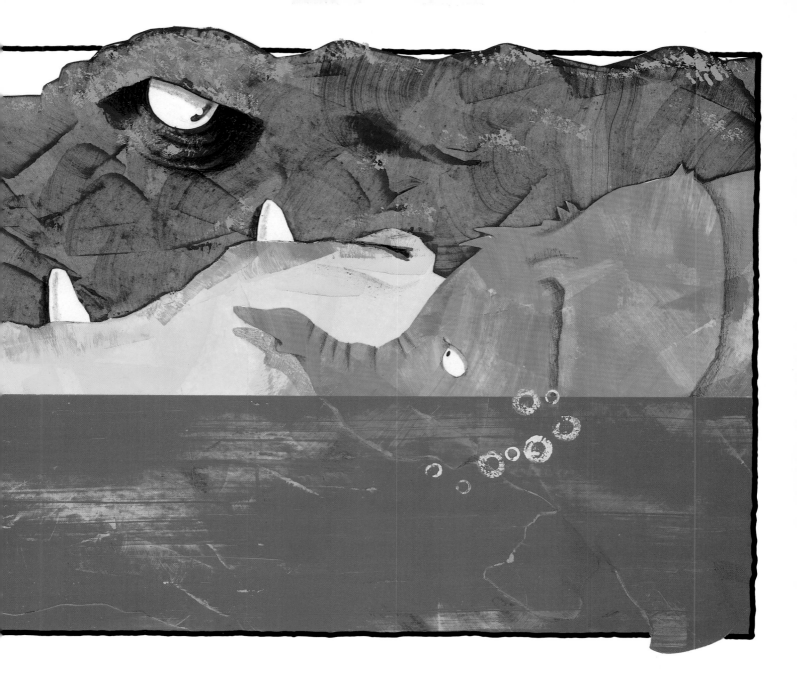

But the bright green croc just swam away,
And didn't even smile.

"If only I were beautiful," said the
Elephant in despair,

As the butterfly flapped its gleaming
Wings and fluttered in the air.

But then one day the elephant saw
A rainbow shining bright.

She traveled far until she stood
In its shafts of colored light.

"At least I'm bright while I stand here,"
Said the elephant with a sigh.

But she knew it wouldn't really last.
And a tear rolled from her eye.

She wandered home, her head hung low,
Still feeling very sad.

She didn't know that she should be
Content with what she had.

Her friends soon came to gather round.
They came from near and far.

They said, "You surely know we love you
Just the way you are."

And though her skin's still dull and gray,
She holds herself with pride.